UNITED STATES LINES

S.S. UNITED STATES Sailing _____ at _____ (local New York City time)

Class FIRST from Pier No. 86 North River, foot of West 6th St., New York City

EMBARKATION FROM _____ M. to _____ M.

on _____
(DAY)

_____
(DATE)

HEAVY BAGGAGE SHOULD ARRIVE AT PIER DAY PREVIOUS TO SAILING

IMPORTANT

PASSPORTS—BE SURE YOUR PASSPORT IS VALID—Passengers are requested to carefully examine their passports to be certain they are valid for travel. Each passport must also contain any required visa at the time it is presented, together with the passage ticket, at the Passenger Desk on the pier prior to embarkation.

SAILING PERMITS (Income Tax Clearance)—Sailing Permits are not required of United States citizens, non-citizens admitted on a B-2 visa who have not been in the United States more than 60 days, or non-citizens transiting the United States within 5 days. Non-citizens in other categories must obtain this document from Collectors of U. S. Internal Revenue in the districts in which they have been residing.

BAGGAGE—The Company's liability for baggage is strictly limited, and passengers are strongly urged to protect themselves against loss by insurance, which may be purchased at any of the Company's agencies or offices.

CAUTION—Passengers are requested to be careful to deliver their baggage into the hands of the Company's representatives only.

PROTECT YOUR TRAVEL FUNDS BY PURCHASING TRAVELERS CHECKS

Free Pass to the Museum

This book entitles one child free admission to a designated maritime museum. (See sticker on front cover.)

Have this page validated at the museum to begin your adventure.

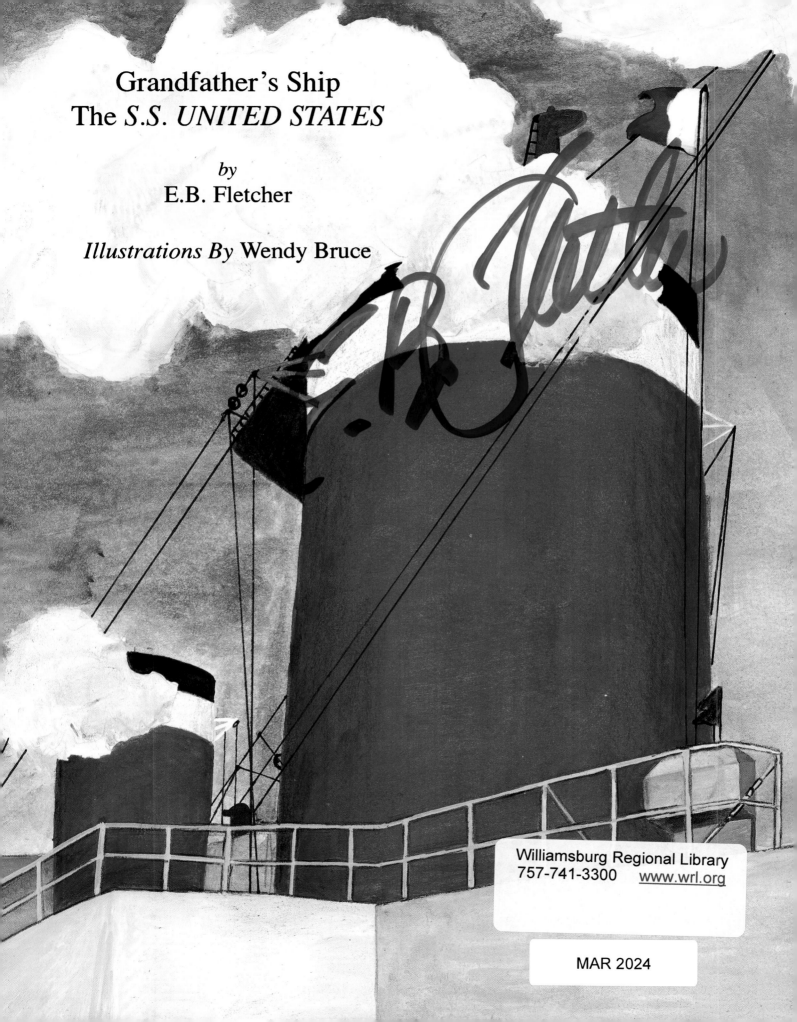

Grandfather's Ship
The *S.S. UNITED STATES*

by
E.B. Fletcher

Illustrations By Wendy Bruce

Library of Congress Control Number 00-091085
ISBN 09701870-0-9

Printed and bound in Spain by Bookprint, S.L., Barcelona

ACKNOWLEDGEMENTS

I would be remiss if I did not thank those who are responsible for the conception of this book. I would like to thank my editor, Charlie Finley, for his guidance and support, Wert Smith, of Dietz Press, for believing in the project, Captain Allan Lonschein and Pat Perez, Maritime Industry Museum, for their help and research, the Mariners' Museum staff, Mike Alexander, for his support and guidance, Jason Buck, for his computer know how, my instructional staff for their patience, Cabell Sale, for introducing me to the Commodore, and my mother, for instilling my love of the sea.

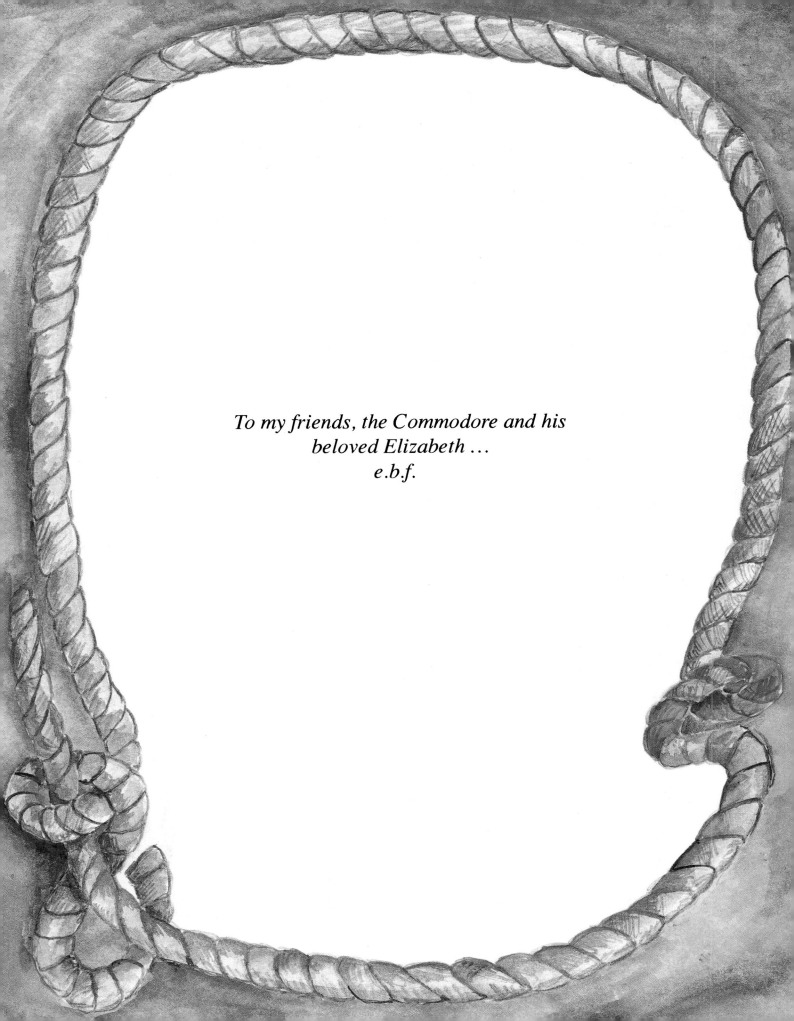

To my friends, the Commodore and his
beloved Elizabeth …
e.b.f.

TABLE OF CONTENTS

CHAPTER ONE

"Your grandfather is coming to see us this weekend, Jon! He and Grandma Liz will be here tomorrow afternoon when you come home from school!" said Mama.

"Oh! Boy!" yelled Jon, jumping up and down. "Mama, do you think Grandfather and I can go down to see the ships?"

"You'll have to ask him, Jon, but I don't see why not."

"Even the lonely ship?" asked Jon.

Mama sighed and said, "You'll have to ask him. Now, run upstairs and wash up for dinner."

Jon ran up the stairs taking two at a time. He scooted the wooden stool over to the sink in the bathroom and leaned over to turn on the faucet. "I can't wait until I'm seven years old," thought Jon to himself. "Then, maybe I'll be old enough not to need this ol' stool anymore."

At school on Friday, Jon had art class and he painted a water-colored picture using black, red, blue and white paints. When he got home from school he saw Grandfather's white Lincoln parked in front of the house. Jon ran up the front steps, burst through the door and, clutching his picture, dashed into the living room where Grandfather and Grandma Liz were seated. Jon scrambled up into Grandfather's awaiting arms still clutching his water-colored picture.

Grandfather lifted Jon high in the air. "Why, Jon my boy! Let me get a good look at you! Haven't seen you in several months!" Jon squealed with delight as Grandfather held him up in the air.

"Roy!" said Grandma Liz sternly. "Put him down! You're going to scare him or worse, drop him!"

"No he's not Grandma," said Jon laughing. "I like it!"

"You see Liz," said Grandfather swinging Jon back down to the floor.

"Look Grandfather!" said Jon. "I painted you a picture today in art class!"

"They have art classes in first grade now, do they?" inquired Grandfather.

"Uh-huh," giggled Jon as Grandfather leaned down and tickled him. Grandfather sat back down in the wing chair by the fireplace and studied the picture that Jon had drawn. As Grandfather gazed at the picture, he looked at Jon who

was grinning from ear to ear with anticipation of approval. "It's the lonely ship, Grandfather," said Jon. "The one at Penn's Landing." Grandfather looked at Jon and then pondered the drawing. Grandfather's eyes grew distant and a faint sadness caused them to become dark.

Grandma Liz got up from her chair and stood behind Grandfather and gazed at the art work. She patted Grandfather on the shoulder and smiled at Jon.

"Dinner's ready!" called Mama as she brought out steaming plates of spaghetti from the kitchen. "Jon, run up and wash your hands." Jon scrambled from the room and up the wide set of stairs.

At dinner, Jon asked Grandfather, "Can we go to the naval base and look at the ships?"

Grandma Liz smiled at Grandfather. Grandfather hesitated a moment, leaned over and tousled Jon's hair and said, "Why sure."

Jon grinned and said, "YYEESSS!!!" while looking heavenward. Then he looked at the faces before him as if suddenly remembering something and said, "And the lonely ship too?"

Grandfather was silent for a moment, giving Grandma Liz time to speak. "You cleaned your plate well tonight Jon! I think spaghetti is one of your favorites!"

"I was hungry," said Jon, wiping his mouth with the linen dinner napkin. "I didn't eat much lunch today. They had mystery meat again!"

Grandma Liz laughed and said, "Well, Evelyn baked you some of those chocolate chip cookies you love! How about some for dessert?"

Grandfather cleared his throat, "I think I'd like some of those! How about you, sport?"

"Sure, Grandfather!"

As Grandmother and Mama cleared the plates from the dining room table, Mama asked, "How is dear ol' Evelyn doing? Does she still keep house for you or has she gone to part-time?"

"Oh darlin' she comes when she can. She still does the ironing. Nothing gets real dirty anymore."

As Mama took some plates into the kitchen she called out to Grandma Liz, "Leave Jack's place set. He'll be late comin' home from work."

Jon leaned over to Grandfather and whispered, "Daddy's working on a big project, and he's got to have it ready by Monday."

"Oh!" said Grandfather. "Well, we'll keep you busy so Dad can work, huh?"

"Okay, Grandfather."

CHAPTER TWO

Saturday afternoon's weather was sunny and bright with cool temperatures making the early spring air crisp. Jon and Grandfather climbed into the Lincoln and off they went to the naval base to look at the retired fleet. After they had parked the car, Grandfather and Jon walked dockside looking at the ghostly gray hulks as seagulls glided softly overhead.

Jon asked, "What do ya' call ships like these?"

"They're called mothballed," responded Grandfather.

"Like when Mama puts mothballs in my sweaters?"

"Something like that," chuckled Grandfather. They walked a little further on, then Grandfather said, "See that ship? That's a frigate. And, see the guns on that one? Battleship, my boy. Those guns are massive and can do a lot of damage."

"How come you know so much about these ships?" asked Jon.

Grandfather smiled and said, "Because I served on several ships such as these during the war!"

"WOW! You never told me that before, Grandfather. Tell me about them."

Grandfather looked down at the ground for a moment, sighed, and then looked up at a radar mast on the nearest ship. "That was a long time ago, Jon."

Jon slipped his tiny hand into Grandfather's as they continued to walk along. Jon lovingly looked into Grandfather's blue weathered eyes and said, "Please tell me about the ships, Grandfather."

Grandfather smiled. As they slowly walked dockside of the mothballed fleet, Grandfather told Jon about being in the naval reserve and sailing the Pacific. "One of the first ships that I was on was called the *MELVILLE*. We sailed out of Pearl Harbor, in Hawaii, and later to the Caribbean. After that, I took command of the *LIVINGSTON* in San Francisco. That ship was true navy with its crew."

Jon was hanging on every word. "WOW! Grandfather! You took command? You mean, like a pirate?"

Grandfather stopped walking and looked down at his tiny grandson. "What! Pirate?" Then, began to laugh. "No, nothing like that. Taking command of a ship means that you're the C.O., the Captain; you're in charge!"

"OH! I get it," said Jon nodding his head. "What other ships did you go on?"

"Well, let's see. There was the *GAGE*. Then, as well as I can remember, the *GENERAL LEROY ELTINGE*."

"Hey!" said Jon stopping in his tracks. "You had a ship that had your name, Leroy!" Grandfather nodded his head in agreement and said, "Well, yes our first names are the same." As they walked along, Grandfather's voice became softer and softer as he reflected on his days at sea. Then he and Jon just quietly continued.

After a while Jon said, "Are you sad?"

Grandfather cleared his throat and looked lovingly down at his grandson and replied, "Yes, I guess."

"Why?"

"Because," said Grandfather, "These ships here were built to protect our country in the event of war. And, it's a good thing to protect our country, but war, Jon is a very sad event. A lot of people die when there's a war and so it makes me sad."

Jon asked, "Did you know people who died when it was war?"

"Yes, I did."

"Do you miss them?"

"Oh yes," said Grandfather. "But those people that I knew, are safe now and they won't hurt anymore."

"You mean because they are in heaven with Jesus?"

"Yes, Jon," said Grandfather.

"I don't want you to be sad."

Grandfather smiled at him and said, "There are a lot of things about life that can make you sad. But, there are a lot that can make you happy too."

"Like snowflakes?" asked Jon.

"Snowflakes?"

"Yeah! Snowflakes make me happy!"

Grandfather threw his head back and laughed. He put his arm around Jon and pulled him close as they walked along; then Grandfather said, "There were other ships that I sailed on and they didn't have as much to do with war. Those ships make me happy."

"What other ships, Grandfather?"

"Well there was the *WASHINGTON, MANHATTAN, AMERICA* and ... well, good ships. Say, all of this talking and walking is making me hungry! How about you and me getting ourselves some ice cream?"

"That sounds good," said Jon, as they made a loop around the docks back to where they had parked.

"It's getting kinda' close to dinner. See, my Mickey Mouse watch says it's 4 o'clock." Jon held his arm up so that Grandfather could see.

"That's all right," replied Grandfather chuckling. "We'll still get some ice cream."

Jon looked sheepishly and asked, "Can I get two scoops?"

Grandfather smiled and said, "I think that it'll be all right."

"We don't have to tell Mama about this do we?"

Grandfather winked, "No, I think this one can be our secret."

As they walked to the car, Jon pointed and said, "Look! There are two white cars just alike! Which one is yours?"

Grandfather squinted his eyes and after adjusting his glasses said, "The one that says: Big U-2. See? On the license plate?"

"Big U-2?" echoed Jon. "What's that?"

Grandfather looked over in the direction of the Walt Whitman Bridge and said, "A nickname for a lady I knew many years ago."

"You better not let Grandma Liz know about that!" Jon said with eyes and mouth wide open.

"I shouldn't, huh?"

"Nope, she'll be jel ...., 'um jel ...."

"Jealous?" asked Grandfather.

"Yeah, jealous," said Jon.

"Okay," Grandfather chuckled to himself. "I won't tell her. Now, how about some ice cream?"

"Yeah Boy!!" said Jon as he hopped into the front seat with Grandfather buckling him in.

CHAPTER THREE

On the way back from the ice cream shop, Jon sat in the front seat licking a double scoop chocolate ice cream cone. "Are we going to Penn's Landing to see the other ship now? You know, the one that's lonely?" Grandfather looked at Jon. "Lonely?"

"Yeah," replied Jon. "There aren't any ships near her so she's got to be lonely. The gray ships have each other to keep them company." Grandfather gripped the steering wheel tightly and with a firm set jaw said, "Huh! We've got to get back! Your mom and Grandma Liz will wonder where we've been!!"

"But Grandfather! The lonely ship is my favorite!!"

Grandfather looked down at his grandson and his firm jaw melted. He sighed and said, "Okay, sport. But, we'll have to be quick."

Jon nodded his head in agreement as he finished up the last of his ice cream and began to crunch the cone. As he munched away, his eyes were fixed on spotting the lonely ship he liked so much.

As Grandfather and Jon drove slowly down Delaware Avenue, the black hull, white superstructure and enormous red, white and blue funnels of an aged luxury liner began to show over the top of the warehouses and buildings near where the ship was moored. Her exterior paint was faded, cracked and flaking. Portholes were broken and deck railings were bent or missing altogether. The lifeboats were gone as well. Grandfather pulled over and parked the car as Jon said, "See! She's got to be lonely! I like to roll the window down and talk to her. I keep her company."

Grandfather turned off the motor and got out of the car. Jon unbuckled himself, opened the door and followed him. They walked quietly up to the chain link fence surrounding the restricted area. As Jon began chattering away … Grandfather's mind took him back to the summer of '52 as he gazed at the ship in front of him. Amid flags flying and the spray of fireboats and well wishing from small harbor craft, Grandfather remembered the sleek new liner entering the port of New York for the first time. She was the golden girl … the pride of the United States Lines and the United States Merchant Marine fleet. Dazzling paint, pennant flags waving … she was captivating!!

9

Jon looked up at his grandfather and said, "Don't you wish you could go on her?"

Grandfather just stared ahead. "Grandfather … Hey! Grandfather?" Still Grandfather gazed ahead. Jon tugged on Grandfather's woolen coat pocket. "Grandfather? Hey … Grandfather?"

Grandfather, suddenly realizing that someone was calling him said, "Huh? Hum? What?"

Jon repeated himself and said, "Wouldn't you like to go on her?"

Grandfather abruptly backed away from the gates surrounding them, and clearing his throat announced in a commanding voice, "We've got to get underway!!"

Jon was puzzled. "Okay, Grandfather." Jon looked into his Grandfather's steel blue eyes and saw tears.

Grandfather walked briskly back to the car, pulling the collar of his tweed coat up near his chin. The wind had begun to pick up. Jon watched his grandfather suspiciously. As the wind whistled around them, Jon thought he heard a voice call to him. It sounded like a lady's voice. He stood still and listened.

"Grandfather, did you hear that?"

"What?"

Jon looked slowly back at the ship then at his grandfather. "Oh … nothing. He climbed into the car while Grandfather buckled him in. All the while, Jon was staring at the ship. Again, he could faintly hear a voice calling to him. Jon couldn't stop looking back at the ship as they drove away from the docks. He kept looking back until the ship was out of sight.

CHAPTER FOUR

On the drive back to the house Jon and Grandfather were quiet and reflective. When they walked through the front door, Grandma Liz called out, "Roy? Is that you? Where have you two been? I've been worried sick! It's getting colder and Jon didn't have on his hat!"

Jon and Grandfather looked at each other and giggled softly. Jon covered his mouth with his hand. Grandfather leaned over and pulling a handkerchief from his pocket said, "Here, let me wipe that smudge of chocolate from your chin. We don't want to spend the night in the brig! The Commodoress would see to it!"

Jon giggled again as Grandfather winked at him and gave him an impromptu spit bath. Grandma Liz came into the foyer wearing an apron, which was not a sight seen often. Jon looked at Grandma in disbelief. She hugged Grandfather and said, "Get your coats off and wash up. I'm fixin' dinner cause Barbara isn't feeling well. It should be ready in about ten minutes." Grandfather questioningly looked at Grandma. Reading his mind, she said, "Oh nothing to worry about, she'll be okay in a couple more months."

Grinning, Grandfather hung up his coat and then helped Jon with his. As they climbed the steps, Jon asked Grandfather, "Does Grandma Liz like to cook?"

"Why do you ask that?"

"Cause, I've never seen her in an apron. Evelyn's always cookin' when I'm at your house."

Grandfather smiled, "She doesn't really like to, but she does know how."

"Oh!" said Jon skipping up the stairs. Jon and Grandfather went into the bathroom to wash up. Jon scooted his wooden stool over to the sink so that he could reach to wash his hands. As Jon was lathering up, he said to Grandfather, "You know, I'm hopin' that when I'm seven, I won't need this ol' stool anymore."

Grandfather laughed as he and Jon rinsed their soapy hands. "When you grow up, Jon, a lot of things will happen. Don't rush it. Try and enjoy being small and that stool. Had a stool like that myself once."

At dinner that night, Jon relayed to his attentive audience all about the sights that he and Grandfather had seen, taking particular care to omit the trip to the ice cream store.

Sunday was a typical lazy day. In the morning, they went to Mass and then out to eat. After lunch, Jon climbed in Grandfather's lap with one of his favorite books and they read together. Jon liked to leaned against Grandfather, feeling the warmth and security of this strong man. Whenever they read together, which hadn't been very often, Grandfather would give Jon peppermint lifesavers as a treat for not missing too many words. Jon hadn't missed but two words today so Grandfather had given him a whole pack!

That evening when Jon was in bed after having his bath, Mama came into his room and tucked him into bed. She kissed Jon and listened to his prayers.

"Jon, you know that Grandfather and Grandma Liz are leaving tomorrow. They're going to get up and eat breakfast with us and then go."

"I'll miss them," said Jon.

"I'll miss them, too. But, they'll return on Friday on their way back from New York. You'll have that to look forward to, right?"

"Yeah … okay. Mama?"

"Hmmm?" replied Mama as she closed the blinds and turned on his night light.

Jon hesitated and said, "Why does the lonely ship upset Grandfather?"

Mama turned around and looked questioningly at Jon. "Why would you think that, sweetie?"

"Because when he looks at it, he gets funny."

"Funny?"

"Yeah, he had raindrops in his eyes like I do when I'm sad."

Mama was now by Jon's bed and she sat down quietly and said, "When did Grandfather have raindrops in his eyes?"

"When we went to see the lonely ship yesterday."

"I see," said Mama looking distracted.

"Mama, why is Grandfather sad about it?"

Mama looked Jon in the eye and said, "I think you need to ask Grandfather. He will tell you if YOU ask him."

"Does Grandfather love the ship?"

Mama's eyes filled with love for her young son and she said, "Well, we love

12

people not things. But, sometimes things, like the ship, take on so many memories of people that I guess, we think they're real."

"But, the lonely ship is real, Mama. She talked to me yesterday."

"She did?" said Mama, fluffing Jon's pillow and tucking him under the covers.

"Yeah," said Jon. "I didn't hear exactly what she said but, she said something."

Mama stroked Jon's head and said, "Then, you must listen carefully next time so that you can hear exactly what she says."

"Okay, Mama."

Daddy came and stood in the doorway watching Mama tuck Jon in. "Can I come in, or is this conversation private?"

"Come on in, sweetie," Mama said.

"Good night, slugger," said Daddy walking over to Jon and kissing him on the forehead.

"Night Daddy," replied Jon as he snuggled down in the covers with his sailor bear.

CHAPTER FIVE

On Friday afternoon before Jon got home, Grandfather and Grandma Liz arrived from their visit in New York. While Grandfather was resting from the trip, Grandma Liz helped mother set the table for supper. "Liz," said Mama. "Jon told me about going with Ajax (that's what Mama called Grandfather because his ships had always been so clean) to Penn's Landing last Saturday. Did Ajax say anything to you about it?"

"No," replied Grandma Liz, looking concerned.

"Jon told me that Ajax had tears in his eyes when he saw the ship, and Jon didn't understand that of course."

"Ah," sighed Grandma Liz. "It tears Roy up to see the ship so neglected, abused and rejected. Oh, darlin' she was a beauty! You should have seen her …those wonderful red, white and blue smokestacks, the racing black hull … she was the fastest liner of her time. And, oh the celebrities that she carried to and from Europe! John Wayne, Jimmy Stewart, the Duke and Duchess of Windsor…" Grandma looked at Mama sadly. She was quiet for a moment. "Harry Manning, her first Commodore, John Anderson, her second … They're all gone now. Even Mr. Gibbs, her designer, is gone. Roy remembers it all … he is her last Commodore; one of the few left to see her horrible fate alone. And, there's nothing we seem to be able to do about the situation. It's funny. People can't get enough about shipwrecks and death, but a liner which had an impeccable record, nothing!"

Mama stood looking at Grandma and said, "Jon is asking a lot of questions about Ajax and the ship. I think he needs to know. Could you talk to Ajax and see if he'll tell Jon her history?"

Grandma closed her eyes for a moment, opened them and said to Mama, "I'll do my best."

Mama hugged Grandma and said, "You ARE the Commodoress you know!"

Grandma Liz chuckled, "Oh, go on!"

CHAPTER SIX

Jon was up bright and early on Saturday morning eating his favorite cereal, Captain Crunch, and watching reruns of Bugs Bunny cartoons. He had dressed himself and had done a fairly good job except that he still got confused sometimes about which feet his shoes went on. He didn't think that was SO bad. "At least," he said to himself, "I know how to tie 'em." Jon put his breakfast dishes in the sink, as Mama had always instructed, went upstairs and knocked softly on Grandfather and Grandma's door. At first there was no response but, then Jon heard his grandparents stirring. Grandma said, "Come in."

Jon opened the door very quietly so as not to disturb his parents and tip-toed into the bedroom. Grandfather and Grandma Liz were in bed talking quietly. Grandfather hauled Jon up in bed and nestled him between his grandparents.

Grandfather said, "Sport, it's only 7:30! What are you doin' dressed?"

Jon replied, "I'm ready to go see the ship, Grandfather. I'm excited! I watched my 'tunes and had some cereal. Now, I'm ready!"

Grandma Liz smiled and said, "I think I'll go take a nice hot shower and leave you two to talk."

Jon looked at Grandfather and said, "What do 'ya want to talk about Grandfather?"

Grandfather sat up in bed, stared ahead for a moment and then looked at his grandson. "Jon," he said, "You like that ship … the one you call the lonely ship."

"Uh-huh," nodding his head.

"Yeah, I like her too," said Grandfather.

Jon looked questioningly at his grandfather and said, "Her? How come you called the ship, her?"

"Well," said Grandfather, "A long time ago before ladies like your Mama or Grandma were able to go to sea, men missed them so, they named their ships after them."

"I never knew that. So, the lonely ship IS a lady ship and that's why I heard that lady's voice when I went to see her last Saturday. It WAS the lonely ship who talked to me!"

Grandfather looked at Jon and said, "Jon, boy, what are you talking about?"

Jon said, "The lonely ship, Grandfather; she talked to me last Saturday. I told you I heard somethin' in the wind!"

"What did she say?"

Jon said, "I'm not sure. Mama said that I needed to listen better so I'd know what she said. I guess I didn't listen too good. The lonely ship is an old lady ship, isn't she?"

Grandfather looked down at him and said, "That's right. She's pretty old as far as ships go."

Jon thought for a moment and said, "You're old too, Grandfather, aren't 'ya?"

Grandfather grinned at Jon. "Some days I feel older than I really am."

Jon continued, "Are you older than the ship?"

"Yes indeed! I'm older than she is."

Jon thought for a moment and then said, "Say, I don't even know that ship lady's name."

Grandfather smiled and said, "Jon, every ship has a name. The ship's name is usually written on the bow and stern. The lonely ship's name is the *UNITED STATES*."

Jon's mouth and eyes were wide open. "Grandfather, you know her name!"

Grandfather settled back against his pillows and put his arm around him. "Jon, I was the captain of the lonely ship." Jon was speechless. Grandfather continued, "I took command of that ship in 1964 and I was with her right until the time that she was laid up. She was for many years in Norfolk and then, briefly at Newport News and, after being towed to Turkey and the Ukraine, she came to stay here in Philadelphia. I sailed many voyages on that ship. And, well, it is very upsetting to me to see her looking the way she does now. You should have seen her when she was new! What a beauty she was! She was a very clean ship. In all of her years at sea, she never had a breakdown. You could stand on the stern and see her wake for miles! She won the Hales Trophy for the fastest transatlantic crossing! You know, she was built at Newport News Ship-building near where your grandmother and I live." Grandfather was quiet for a bit and Jon was trying to take in all of the information he had just heard.

"This is awesome, Grandfather! Why didn't 'ya tell me this stuff before?"

Grandfather looked at his tiny grandson and said, "I wasn't sure you'd un derstand but, now I know that you do."

Jon looked at Grandfather and said, "Mama says that we love people not things. But, I do love the ship even though it's not a person."

Grandfather hesitated for a moment and then said, "How would you like to go on the lonely ship for a tour?"

Jon's eyes became wide and he threw his arms around Grandfather's neck and said, "OH! BOY! Grandfather would I? You're the best Grandfather in the whole world! Wait 'til my friends Mark and George hear about this!" Jon squeezed Grandfather's neck and said, "Do 'ya still have the keys that drive the ship?"

Grandfather laughed and said, "No, Jon, I'm afraid not. But, I do know the man who owns her and I've given him a call and he's made the arrangements so that we may go aboard her."

Jon thought for a moment. "Gosh Grandfather, the lone … I mean the *UNITED STATES* is sure going to be happy to see you again!"

Grandfather sat quietly wondering if he was going to be as glad to see her.

CHAPTER SEVEN

"Oh No!" exclaimed Grandfather. "Look what they have done to her!! This is worse than I had imagined. Liz, look at this!" Jon was still trying to adjust to the lack of light now that they were inside the ship. He looked back at the long ladder that he, Grandfather, Grandma Liz and several other people he didn't know had just climbed up to get into the ship. "The bulkheads are gone," said Grandfather.

"What are bulkheads?" asked Jon.

"Walls," responded Grandfather. "They were removed several years ago to get rid of the asbestos in them."

Jon asked, "What's sestus?"

Grandfather with hands on hips looked around and said, "Asbestos, Jon. It's a substance that was used to make the ship fire resistant. But, it was found to cause cancer in people, so it was removed from the ship."

"Oh!" said Jon.

Grandma Liz stood next to Grandfather shaking her head at the sight before them. Grandfather began to get his bearings, bulkheads or not, and proceeded to give a guided tour through the ship showing Jon and the others where things used to be. Eventually, the tour made its way to the bridge. Grandfather stood in the wheelhouse, the place from which he commanded his sailors and navigated through the mighty Atlantic. As he spoke of his years at sea, his voice never cracked but tears brimmed in his eyes to see his once grand lady in such a feeble state. Grandma Liz held his hand never saying a word. Grandfather showed Jon where the captain's chair, the engine telegraph and radar equipment used to be. The wheelhouse had been completely stripped.

As Grandfather spoke to the others and answered their questions, Jon walked onto the bridge-wing. He looked up into the overcast sky and watched the seagulls dance in the air above him. The wind began to pick up as Jon stood quietly. He was actually standing on the lonely ship! He was HERE! And, since he hadn't known what the ship looked like in her heyday, he was not disappointed in her appearance now. "I think you're still beautiful! You'll always be beautiful to me, *UNITED STATES!*" The wind began to blow more. Again, Jon heard a lady's voice speak to him. This time it was not as faint. He stood and listened as his Mama had told him to.

"You came, Jon! You came to see me and you brought my Commodore! Thank-you, Jon! Thank You!" Jon stood wide eyed. He knew he'd heard her really heard her. She was REAL! She had REAL thoughts, REAL feelings and perhaps even REAL emotions!

"Jon, are you ready to go down to the engine room now? I'll show you the best engines ever put in a luxury liner!" said Grandfather.

"Yeah, Grandfather. I'm ready." Grandma Liz took Jon's hand and guided him through the dark shadows of the once proud liner.

In the engine room, Jon saw gauges, nozzles, hoses and even a fire extinguisher. This part of the ship looked normal as if at any time the crew would announce that she was underway. One of the men on the tour asked, "Did you ever know how fast the Big U could really go?"

Grandfather replied, "Her speed was top secret; however we never fully opened up the boilers to capacity to see just exactly what she could do. So, the answer to your question is no. Best estimate was around 40 knots."

Jon tugged on Grandfather's coat. "Grandfather, did he say Big U?"

Grandfather smiled. "That's the ship's nickname."

Jon grinned, realizing now who the mystery lady in Grandfather's life really was. He continued to pull on Grandfather's coat and ask questions as they toured the ship. Grandfather was very patient and responded to all of Jon's inquiries. After the tour was complete and everyone was dockside, Jon looked up at the enormous black hull in front of him. He said softly, "I hope you can dream about being at sea the way it used to be. Maybe that will help you not to be so sad and lonely."

As Jon followed Grandfather and Grandma to the car, he looked back at the ship and he heard her faintly say, "My dreams of years gone by are all that I have now. You've given me another memory, today's visit! Thank-you, little one!"

Jon stopped in his tracks and said out loud, "You're welcome!" Grandma and Grandfather both stopped walking, turned around and Grandfather said, "Who are you talking to?"

Jon said, "The ship of course. She thanked me for coming to see her and bringing you."

Grandfather and Grandma looked around questioningly at each other while Jon came skipping up to his grandparents and took them both by the hand.

That night at supper, Jon retold his parents every bit of his adventures on the ship that day. Mama had ordered pizza, so they sat around the toasty fire in the fireplace and ate. Later, while Mama and Daddy tucked Jon in and listened to his prayers, Jon said, "Mama, I left out one part of the trip today."

"What part is that, sweetie?" asked Mama.

"You know how you told me to listen better the next time the ship talked to me?"

"Um-hum," said Mama kneeling by her son's bed.

"Well, she talked to me today and I listened real good!"

"What did she say?" asked Mama.

"She thanked me for comin' to see her and bringing Grandfather."

"Oh?" Mama looked amused.

"Did you thank your grandparents for taking you today?" asked Daddy.

"Oh, yeah," said Jon. "I had real good manners like you told me."

"Good boy!" said Daddy ruffling Jon's hair.

"Jon," asked Mama, "Did Grandfather get raindrops in his eyes today?"

"Yeah," answered Jon, "When we went in the wheelhouse."

"Umm," said Mama looking up at Daddy with concern. "We better get you to sleep!" Jon yawned widely. "I love you, sweetie. Pleasant dreams." Daddy went into his study to work for awhile, but Mama tip-toed down the hall and knocked on Grandfather and Grandma Liz's door.

"Come in," said Grandma.

Mama came in and saw that Grandfather and Grandma were in their pajamas and already in bed. Mama came over and kissed Grandfather on the cheek.

"Well, what's that for?" he asked.

"For being unselfish and giving your grandson a day he'll remember for the rest of his life. I know it was difficult for you to see the ship today," said Mama. Grandfather nodded, smiled and hugged Mama back. She kissed Grandma Liz. Grandma took Mama's hand and just squeezed it and winked. Mama winked back.

Grandfather asked, "Is Jon asleep?"

Mama said, "If he's not yet, he should be shortly. He was exhausted!" Grandfather laughed and nodded in agreement. "I'm pretty tired myself." "Well," said Mama, "I'll let you get your sleep. Good night!" "Good night," echoed Grandfather and Grandma.

CHAPTER EIGHT

During Jon's spring vacation, he visited his grandparents for an entire week. They went to the Mariners' Museum and spent hours looking at the ship models and exhibits. His favorite room was the Gibbs' wing, named for William Francis Gibbs, with so many items from the *UNITED STATES!* Grandma Liz pointed out to Jon the various items that she and Grandfather had donated to the museum including a life-ring with the ship's name on it. Jon's grandparents took him to Nag's Head for lunch one day where they dined at Wind Mill Point. Jon was fascinated by the furniture, pictures and other memorabilia from the *UNITED STATES.* Grandfather introduced Jon to the owner of the restaurant and she gave him a tee-shirt with a picture of the ship on the back of it! Jon took walks to the yacht club with Grandma Liz, and he and Grandfather got ice cream and sat watching the ships in Hampton Roads. When it was time for him to leave, Grandfather presented Jon with a framed picture of himself in his captain's uniform standing on the bridge-wing of the *UNITED STATES.* Jon wouldn't put it in his suitcase; he held it in his lap the whole way home.

On June 26th, Grandfather and Grandma came to visit. School was out and Jon was getting ready to have his seventh birthday! He was so excited because he and Grandfather shared the same birthday and they usually celebrated together. So many things were happening! Mama was getting ready to have a new baby, Grandfather and Grandma Liz were planning to take him to visit Grandfather's college at Fort Schuyler, and he had grown a whole inch; he was sure he wouldn't need his stool anymore!

Jon had the traditional birthday party with his friends, cake, ice cream, balloons and games. After the party was over, Grandfather came into Jon's room where he was playing with some of his new toys.

"Hey, sport," said Grandfather, "Having fun?"

"Yeah, Grandfather," said Jon, "Tonight you get your new toys!"

Grandfather laughed and said, "Well, I don't know about toys. Maybe a shirt or two. Listen, sport, your Grandmother and I wanted to wait and give you our present so, here you go!" Grandma appeared in the doorway and watched

as Jon carefully unwrapped a rectangular box, inside was a miniature model of the *UNITED STATES*. Jon's eyes opened wide and he was smiling from ear to ear as he took the model from the box and gingerly held it up.

Grandfather said, "You can always keep her company, Jon. With you around, she'll never be lonely again."

"Oh! Grandfather!" said Jon still staring at the model. "This is like the one you have at your house in the glass case!"

"That's right. Now Jon, this model is valuable and needs to be kept in a safe place. It's not a toy to be played with like your Hot Wheels are, huh?"

"Yes, Sir!" said Jon and he stood up and saluted his Grandfather.

Grandfather chuckled and returned Jon's salute.

"Oh!" said Grandma. "I almost forgot! If you're going to be the master of the ship, then you'll need this!" Placing a child-sized captain's hat on Jon's head.

Jon grabbed his Grandfather by the leg and said, "Thank you for being the best Grandfather!"

That night, they all went out to dinner to celebrate Grandfather's birthday. Last year for Grandfather's ninetieth birthday, Grandma Liz had a huge party at the Mariners' Museum for Grandfather and there had been over three hundred guests! But, this year they were just keeping it simple. Grandfather got several shirts and cards but the item he seemed the most pleased with was a belt with signal flags on it which spelled out his name. When they arrived home, Jon went up and changed into his pajamas and then went into the bathroom to brush his teeth. "Here goes!" he said to himself. He leaned over to turn on the faucet, without using his wooden stool. If he stood on his tip-toes, he could reach! He brushed his teeth and then picked up the wooden stool to carry it to his closet. As Jon picked up the stool, it flipped over so that the underside was facing him. He saw that there was writing on it. Written on the stool were the words: "Happy Birthday, Leroy John Alexanderson, June 27, 1912." Jon placed the stool on the floor and looked at the writing again. Then, he picked up the stool and carried it down the hall to Grandfather and Grandma Liz's room. He knocked softly on the door and Grandma answered. "What have you got there, darlin'?"

"It's my ol' stool. Well, it used to be mine," said Jon.

"Whatever do you mean?" Grandma asked.

"Look!" said Jon, turning the stool over and showing her the writing.

Grandma smiled and said, "Commodore, come here. Jon wants to show you something."

Grandfather came out of the bathroom holding his toothbrush. "What's this?"

Jon answered, "You know I told you that when I was seven, maybe I wouldn't need this anymore. Well, it worked! I'm seven today and if I stand on my tip-toes, I can turn on the water all by myself!"

"OH!" said Grandfather smiling, "I see!"

"Besides," continued Jon, "This is really yours. See, it's got your name on it! Somebody gave it to you for your birthday and since today's your birthday too, I thought I'd give it back to 'ya!"

Grandfather smiled at Jon and said, "I was two years old when I got that stool. That's a very thoughtful thing to do but, I have an idea."

"What?" questioned Jon.

"How about you keeping it and giving it to your new baby brother or sister when they're born?"

Jon thought for a moment, "I hadn't thought of that."

"That's okay," said Grandfather. "It's Grandfather's job to think of things for you sometimes."

Grandma Liz said, "Here, let me help you put that away and then I'll tuck you in, hum?"

"Okay," said Jon.

CHAPTER NINE

The next morning at breakfast, Grandfather didn't come down to eat. "Where's Grandfather?" asked Jon.

"Oh he's still tired from last night's activities," said Grandma. "He'll be down later, I'm sure."

Mama and Daddy looked at each other.

Grandma said, "We'll check on him again after breakfast. He was up and down all night with indigestion."

"Well," said Jon, "I've decided that we need to have a birthday party for the *UNITED STATES!*"

Mama said, "A birthday party?"

"Yeah; she's old like Grandfather and he gets birthdays so why can't we give her one?"

Mama said, "Honey, the *UNITED STATES* was **built;** she wasn't born and it took over a year to build her."

"Oh," said Jon, thinking.

"Hey, why don't you celebrate the date of her maiden voyage?" suggested Grandma Liz.

"What's a maiden voyage?" asked Jon.

"It's the ship's very first trip on a major ocean with all of the passengers on it." answered Grandma Liz.

"Oh!" said Jon. "When was it?"

"Now, let me see. Oh, yes! July 3, 1952."

"Hey," said Jon, "July third is next week! We can pack a picnic lunch and go eat with her!"

"What are you going to give her as a present?" asked Daddy.

"She just likes the company, Papa," said Jon. "She doesn't need a present."

"Oh. Excuse me, I guess you're right!"

Mama said, "Jon, we won't be able to get close to her like before."

"Sure we will. Grandfather will tell them we're coming."

"Sweetie," said Mama looking apologetically to Grandma Liz, "You can't go on the ship every time Grandfather comes to visit. You got to go on board as a treat. You understand? We can't impose on your Grandfather."

Jon wasn't sure what *impose* meant but from the way Mama was looking at him, he thought he shouldn't push it. He pondered for a moment and said, "Could we at least go down and visit her on her birthday and sing to her sittin' in the car?"

"I don't see any harm in that," said Mama.

"Okay. She'll appreciate it!"

CHAPTER TEN

Grandfather stayed in his room sleeping a lot for the next few days. When he was up, he just wasn't himself, so Grandma Liz insisted that he go to the doctor who was one of Daddy's and Mama's friends.

The next day, Jon was playing with his friends, Cabell and Sid, in the backyard when Mama called him to come in for dinner. Jon came in, washed up and sat down at the breakfast room table. "Where is everybody?" inquired Jon looking at only two places set for dinner.

Mama said, "Jon, Grandfather went to the doctor today and he found out that Grandfather's very sick and so the doctor's put him in the hospital. Grandma Liz and Daddy are with him. Daddy has called Nana and Pops to the hospital too."

"Why?" asked Jon. "Can't he just have a shot?"

Mama sighed, "No, sweetie. It's more complicated than that. Grandfather's heart is sick and he hasn't been feeling well for some time. He has to have an operation to help his heart get better."

"Does he have to have the operation?" asked Jon.

"Yes, love, he does."

"I don't think I'm hungry anymore. All of a sudden I have a rock in there," Jon said pointing to his stomach.

"It's okay," said Mama. "You don't have to eat now if you don't want to."

Jon sat in the chair for a moment and looked up at his mother and said, "Mama, is Grandfather going to die?"

Mama hesitated a moment before answering. "Jon, to be honest with you, I don't know. I sure hope not but, you do know that we all have to die sometime. It's part of living."

"What will happen to Grandfather if he dies?" asked Jon.

"Well," said Mama, "His chemical remains, his body, will be here on Earth. But, his soul, his personality, the Grandfather you know and love will go to Heaven to live with God. You won't be able to write to him, call him or e-mail him like you do now but, you will be able to pray for him and ask God to keep him safe in Heaven so you can be together again someday."

Jon sat looking straight ahead out the bay window. His lower lip quivered and a tear streamed down his face. Mama gently turned his chin toward her and Jon saw that her face was very sad.

"Mama, I think I'm getting rain drops." He scrambled up into Mama's lap and began to sob. Mama rocked him and patted him and told him that she loved him. "I don't want Grandfather to go away!"

"I know you don't, sweetie. I don't want him to, either." Mama rocked Jon until he had calmed down. She smoothed his hair, then gave him a tissue to wipe his nose and eyes.

That evening Daddy came home, ate some supper, went upstairs and packed Grandma Liz's smaller suitcase and took it back to the hospital. Grandma wouldn't leave Grandfather's side and she was sleeping at the hospital, too. Daddy said that Grandfather was in the Cardiac Care Unit and that things didn't look good. Mama called the priest, Father Clark, and he came to the hospital to be with Grandma Liz. Mama cleaned house and put fresh sheets on the beds and clean towels in the bathrooms for Nana and Pops. Jon stayed in his room looking at Grandfather's picture and the model of the *UNITED STATES*. Later when he was in bed, Jon decided to pray. He wasn't sure what to ask God for, so he just asked that Grandfather's heart would get better so that he could come home. Jon told God that if Grandfather's getting better wasn't what He wanted, he would try not to be mad at Him. As Jon lay in his bed, it suddenly hit him. "I need to tell the *UNITED STATES* about Grandfather! She'll know what to do! Tomorrow I'll go and tell her."

CHAPTER ELEVEN

Later on that night, Jon was awakened several times by the shrill ring of the telephone, then muffled voices, and footsteps. He was in a dream-like state while all of this was going on. In the morning, he wasn't sure whether it had really happened or whether it had all been just a dream. He got up, dressed, made his bed and he put on his captain's hat. Mama was sitting in a wing chair in the living room. Her eyes were swollen and red and she looked very tired. The house was still. Jon stopped at the foot of the steps and looked at his mother.

"Hi, Honey!" Mama said trying to sound chipper. "Did you sleep well?"

Jon slowly walked over to Mama and said, "Why are you cryin'?"

Mama ignored the inquiry and said, "Hey, I made your favorites, waffles, for breakfast! Let's go get some. Daddy will be back in a few minutes with Nana and Pops. Their flight arrived this morning."

Jon repeated his question, "Why have you been cryin', Mom?"

Mama looked at Jon, her eyes filled with tears and she said, "Oh, sweetie, I'm cryin' because I am very sad. We got some bad news last night."

"Is it about Grandfather?" asked Jon.

Mama looked up at the ceiling and bit her lower lip. She looked down at Jon.

"Yes, sweetie. I'm afraid so."

"Mama, didn't he get his operation?" Mama's tears trickled down her cheeks and she cleared her throat. "No, Jon, he didn't. He wasn't able to have his operation. Grandfather's heart stopped beating. He passed away early this morning."

Jon yelled, "NO! NO!" Mama eased him toward her trying to comfort him but he pulled away from her and ran toward the front door.

"Jon, where are you going? Come back here!" yelled Mama following him.

"Johannes Alexander! Come back here!" yelled Mama again.

Jon went out the front door, took off running through the front yard and down the sidewalk. Tears stung his face as he ran through the foggy summer morning. The sky was dark and overcast and fog hung in the air. Mama screamed

for Jon but he never looked back. She ran inside and went to the phone and called Daddy in his car.

"Jack, Jon knows about Ajax and he took off! He's run away!........No, I don't know where he's gone and I'm in no condition to chase after him!"

Grandma Liz had come home to take a shower and rest. Hearing the commotion downstairs, she came down to see what was wrong. In a moment she was by Mama's side. Mama was half sobbing and yelling about where Jon had gone and why he'd left when Grandma Liz said, "Calm down! I think I know where he might be."

Mama, looking absolutely bewildered, hesitated and said, "You do? Where?"

Grandma said, "You stay here and I'll get him. I don't believe he's gone far." Through all of this Daddy was still on the phone asking what was going on.

"Uh, Honey? Liz says she knows where Jon's gone! She's goin' to get him!" said Mama.

"Where?" yelled Daddy through the phone.

Grandma Liz and Mama looked at each other for a moment and then said at the same time, "The ship!"

Jon's legs hurt, arms hurt and chest hurt but he still kept running until he got to the area with the fence surrounding where the ship was moored. He began to climb the chain link fence and crossed over the barbed wire. It cut his arm and leg and tore his shorts. He ran to the pier and then stood still looking up at the enormous ship in front of him. Jon said breathlessly, "I know it's your birthday … I wanted to have a party for you … but, oh …" Jon fell down on his knees crying. His little body shook all over as tears streamed down his face. Between sobs he said to the ship, "Grandfather was sick … he … had a sick heart … they were … going to give him an … operation … but he couldn't wait. Oh, he's gone UNITED!! He's gone!! My grandfather's gone!!!"

Jon cried while rocking himself back and forth huddled on the pier with his arms around his legs. He stayed that way for quite sometime. He wiped his tears with the back of his hand and looked up at the ship through blurred eyes. The ship was encased in a shawl of fog. Her superstructure could barely be seen except for the bridge and radar mast. Even the funnels were hidden.

The wind picked up and she spoke to him, "Dry your eyes, little one. Commo dore loves you and you loved him. He lives on in you my dear little fellow. He lives on in you … ”

Jon just sat there for what seemed an eternity staring at the ship. He didn't hear the security officers directing Grandma and Daddy to the pier. He didn't see Daddy watching him from behind the fence, nor did he hear the gate open. He wasn't aware of anything until he heard a familiar voice say, "Mind if I join you?" Grandma was staring down at him.

"OH! Grandma!" Jon said hopping to his feet.

"Darlin' are you all right? You've cut yourself! You're bleeding!! And look at your shorts!"

Jon threw himself against his Grandmother. Tears welled up in her eyes. Jon sobbed and said, "I'm so sorry for you, Grandma! I'm so sorry!" Grandma patted Jon's head and held him close. When she had gotten her composure, she knelt down to him so that they were face to face and said, "Commodore is safe. He won't hurt anymore and he's happy now. It's okay, Jon. It's okay. It hurts to lose Grandfather. It's supposed to hurt because we loved him. But, we're all going to be okay!"

"But, Grandma," said Jon. "I didn't even get to say good-bye!"

"I know darlin'." She knelt holding Jon for a while. Finally, Grandma looked at him and said, "You must understand that Grandfather is in paradise. He is with Jesus, God and the angels. Paradise is a wonderful place to be! It's every-thing that makes you happy! It's God's kingdom!"

Jon nodded his head in agreement and said, "Grandma I told the ship about Grandfather and she told me that he lives on 'cause I loved him."

Grandma looked at Jon then slowly turned and looked up at the ship. She turned back to Jon and said, "That's right, darlin'! That's right! Now, let's get you home. You're mom is very worried about you!"

Jon began to walk with Grandma down the pier towards the gate where his father stood. He stopped and looked back at the ship. Through the parting fog, Jon distinctly saw the figure of a man in a captain's uniform standing on the bridge-wing with a pair of binoculars in his hands. Jon blinked, rubbed his eyes and looked again. The figure was gone. Jon turned to his grandmother, "Grandma, could paradise be on the bridge of a ship?"

EPILOGUE

Commodore L.J. Alexanderson is the son of the late Mr. and Mrs. Johannes Alexander Alexanderson who were Swedish immigrants who came to New York in the late 1800s. The Commodore graduated from the New York State Merchant Marine Academy in the early 1930s. He and his wife, Dot, had three children. He began his nautical career in the Pacific on several cargo ships. During the second World War, he commanded several naval vessels and eventually rose to the rank of Rear Admiral in the Naval Reserve. Commodore Alexanderson also served as Commodore of the United States Lines fleet and was captain of several ships of this line, including the *S.S. UNITED STATES*. After the ship was laid up, Commodore went on to command cargo vessels until the mid 1970s when he retired. Sadly, the Commodore's wife, Dot, passed away soon after his retirement.

The Commodore is the last of the United States Merchant Marine officers to hold the rank and title of Rear Admiral and Commodore of the now disbanded United States Lines.

Commodore Alexanderson is alive and well and lives in Hampton, Virginia with his second wife, Elizabeth. He is a much loved and revered gentleman of whom I am greatly fond.

E. B. Fletcher

HIST OR Y OF THE *S.S. UNITED ST ATES*

The *S.S. United States* began as hull number 488 on February 8, 1950 at Newport News Shipbuilding and Dry Dock Company. It would cost an estimated $70 million to build her. She was later christened *"United States"* by Mrs. Tom Connally of Texas on June 23, 1951.

The *United States'* sea trials began on May 14, 1952 off the coast of Virginia. She passed these trials and was delivered to the United States Lines Company on June 21, 1952. The "Big U" arrived in the port of New York for her maiden voyage to a great flotilla of tugs and fireboats giving her an escort to her new home port. Her maiden voyage began on July 3, 1952 with many important people aboard including her designer, William Francis Gibbs. This would be the only voyage he ever took on the ship. He was a very superstitious person.

The *United States* passed Ambrose Light house at 2:36 p.m., the traditional starting point for an east bound chance at the Blue Riband. The ship maintained an average speed of 35 knots on her maiden voyage. She officially captured the Blue Riband for the fastest transatlantic voyage on Monday, July 7, 1952. She had crossed the Atlantic in 3 days, 10 hours and 40 minutes.

Commodore Harry Manning led the ship on her west bound trip as well, and broke another speed record for the return trip. The *United States* crossed the Atlantic in 3 days, 12 hours and 12 minutes at a speed of over 34 knots. As the ship approached Ambrose Light, the ship's band began to play, "I'm Wild About Harry," in tribute to her master.

Harry Manning was a graduate of the New York Nautical School, now known as SUNY Maritime Academy. Her other masters, Commodores Anderson and Alexanderson, also graduated from this school. Commodore Manning was Amelia Earheart's navigator and was on a year's leave when she and her replacement navigator disappeared. Manning was also known as "Rescue Harry" because he had participated in several rescues at sea. Manning commanded the *United States* only a few times.

John Anderson succeeded Manning and became captain of the ship. He eventually rose to the rank of Commodore and was master of the ship until 1964 when he retired. L.J. Alexanderson was then named captain of the super ship and was given the title of Commodore of the United States Lines in July of 1966.

Government subsidies were a necessary part of keeping the *United States* running. In 1969, an extended government subsidy was not renewed, and the only federal money given was $400.00 per passenger ticket sold. The United States Lines couldn't generate the additional money needed to keep the ship running. Between longshoremen's strikes and more passengers flying than sailing, the *United States* was losing more and more money.

After the completion of voyage 400, the ship sailed back to her birthplace of Newport News, Virginia for her annual overhaul. On November 14, 1969, it was announced that the *United States* would be deactivated. She was towed to Norfolk International Terminals on June 19, 1970 and moored at pier 2. She would remain there for the next nineteen years.

The Maritime Administration became the overseers of the ship in the early 1970s until

Richard Hadley, a real estate developer, bought the ship in 1979. He planned to refurbish her and return her to the sea. Plans were drawn, her hull was tested to make sure she was still seaworthy, and her contents were auctioned off to raise money for her costly refurbishment.

In 1989, with still no change in her status, the "Big U" was evicted from her berth at Norfolk and she was again towed across Hampton Roads to an abandoned CSX coal pier.

The ship remained there until June of 1992 when she was towed from her Virginia waters to Turkey. The *United States* had been saved from the scrap heap by Fred Meyer. Mr. Meyer, who sailed on the ship in 1963, bid on her after federal marshalls had seized the ship for lack of payments from Hadley. Meyer, representing Turkish businessmen, bought the ship for over $2 million.

While the ship was in Turkey, she was also taken to the Ukraine and had all of the asbestos removed from her. William Francis Gibbs had made sure that no wood was used on the ship except in the grand pianos and butcher's cutting block. (A friend of mine and I went on her years ago and found wood molding attached to the carpet adhesive in some first class staterooms. Mr. Gibbs would not have liked that!) Everything was aluminum which made the ship light and fire resistant.

Ed Cantor, her owner to date, seized ownership of the *United States* in 1996 and had her towed back to this country from Turkey. Again, the ship had been seized due to lack of payments; this time from the Turkish businessmen. The ship now sits in Philadelphia at pier 52 awaiting her fate.

Several documentary films have been made about the ship, a preservation society has been formed for her and legislation was introduced in Congress for the *United States* to be placed on the National Landmark Register of Historic Places. On June 5, 1999, Commodore Alexanderson received word that registry had been granted.

The *United States* may be globally known but she was "born" in Virginia ... and a Virginian she shall always be.

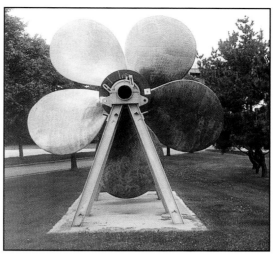

These pictures were taken at the Commodore Leroy J. Alexanderson Park at SUNY Maritime College. The park was dedicated to the Commodore in the fall of 1995. The park contains one of two five blade propellers that were for the *S.S. UNITED STATES*. The ship had four propeller shafts; two shafts used four blade propellers while the other two used five blade propellers. Gibbs & Cox designed the ship this way to increase her underwater speed. The Commodore and Captain Allan Lonschein, Executive Director of the Maritime Industry Museum, were instrumental in seeing that the five blade propeller was donated to the SUNY Maritime College, Bronx, New York. The second propeller is on display at the Mariners' Museum, Newport News, Virginia. These propellers were spares which had been kept at Newport News Shipbuilding and were never used.

A copy of Commodore L.J. Alexanderson's diploma from New York State Merchant Marine Academy which would later become SUNY Maritime College. *(Copy courtesy of Maritime Industry Museum at Fort Schuyler)*

41

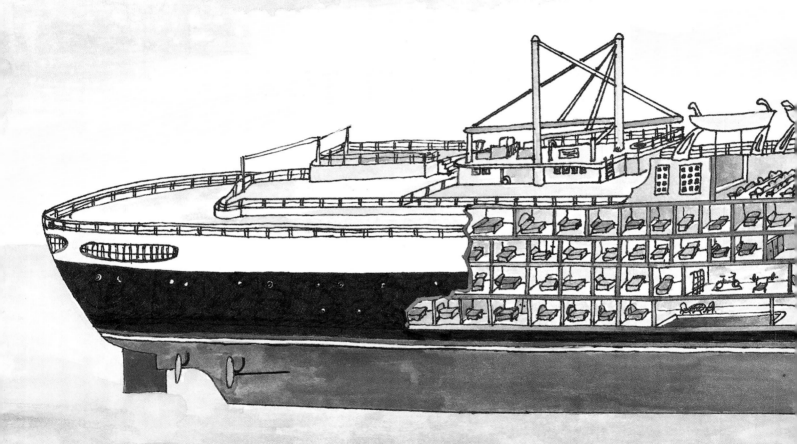

SEVERAL WEB SITES TO VISIT ON THE *UNITED STATES*

- www.ss-united-states.com
- www.mariner.org
- 3n.net/ssunited/ or www.pier90.org/main.htm
- www.nns.com/
- www.users.erols.com/martin/ssus/
- seawifs.gsfc.nasa.gov/SSUS/
- www.SunyMaritime.edu
- www.talking-pages.com/windmillpoint/

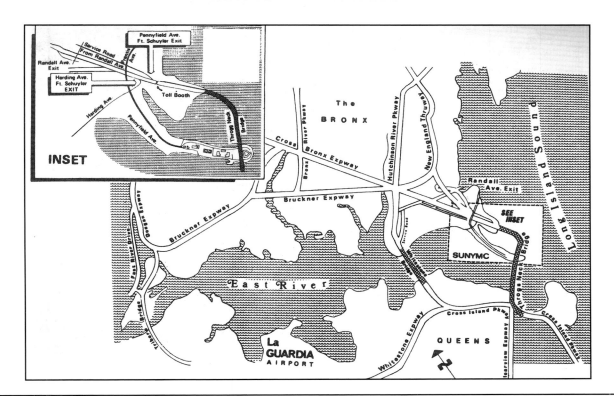

Directions to Fort Schuyler

From Brooklyn or Queens
VIA THE WHITESTONE BRIDGE
Pay toll at extreme right booth, take immediate right exit to traffic light, turn right to next traffic light, turn right then left onto route 295. Keep to right and take "Fort Schuyler" exit, just before Throggs Neck Bridge.

From Manhattan: East Side
North on East River Drive (FDR) to either:
(a) Willis Avenue Bridge (no toll) then keep right to Bruckner Blvd. to ramp leading to Bruckner Expressway, then follow Throggs Neck Bridge signs to Fort Schuyler Exit just before Bridge.
(b) Triborough Bridge ($3.00 toll) follow "New England" signs to Fort Schuyler Exit just before Bridge.

From Manhattan: West Side
North on West Side Highway to 178 St. Exit to I-95 N and Cross Bronx Expressway. Follow Throggs Neck Bridge signs to Fort Schuyler Exit just before Bridge.

From New Jersey
Via George Washington Bridge
Garden State or N.J. Turnpike to New York and I-95 North, then follow signs to Throggs Neck Bridge to Fort Schuyler Exit just before Bridge.

From Upper New York State
and New York State Thruway
After crossing Tappan Zee Bridge, follow I-287 E, then south on Sprain Brook Parkway and Bronx River Parkway to I-95 North. Follow signs to Throggs Neck Bridge and take the Fort Schuyler Exit.

From Hutchinson River Parkway
South to Bruckner Expressway Exit, I-95 South (sharp right after overpass) then follow Throggs Neck Bridge signs to Fort Schuyler Exit on right just before bridge.

From New England and New England Thruway
I-95 South to the Bronx, then follow Throggs Neck Bridge signs to Fort Schuyler Exit on right just before Bridge.

Caution: You must cross three lanes in 300 yards.

From Long Island
and Long Island Expressway
West on Long Island Expressway to Clearview Expressway North to Throggs Neck Bridge; take Pennyfield Avenue—Fort Schuyler Exit immediately after toll station.

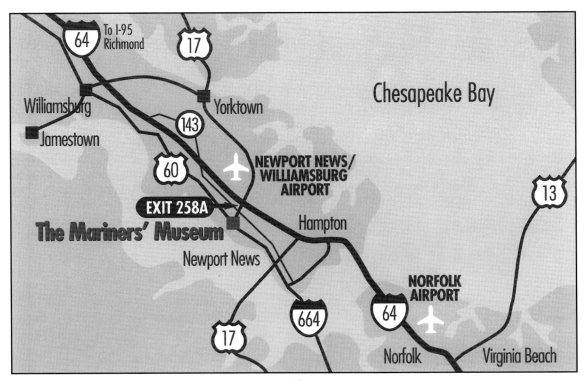

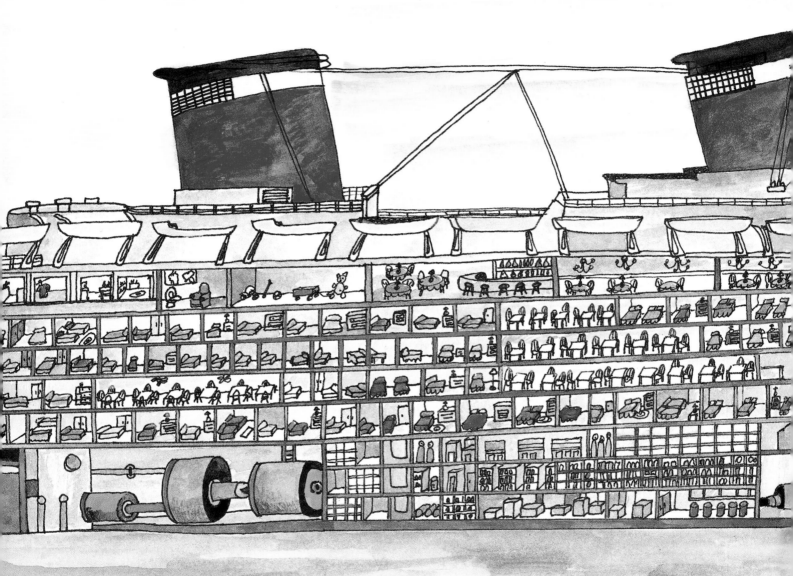

FACTS ABOUT THE *UNITED STATES*

- It took over 3,000 shipyard workers to build the *United States.*
- The only wood aboard the ship was in the butcher's cutting blocks and the grand pianos.
- During her seventeen years in service, 9 babies were born onboard the ship.
- *United States* sailed 2,772,840 nautical miles during her transatlantic career.
- *United States* carried 1,025,691 passengers on transatlantic crossings.

MAIDEN VOYAGE
QUADRUPLE SCREW TURBINE STEAMER
UNITED STATES
Commodore: Harry Manning
Captain, U. S. N. R.

Abstract of Log　　　　　　　　　　　　　　　　　　**Voyage 1, Eastbound**

From NEW YORK to SOUTHAMPTON, via LE HAVRE

DATE	LAT. N.	LONG. W.	NAUT. MILES	SPEED	WIND	REMARKS
July 3						Departure Ambrose L. V. 2:36 p.m., EST
" 4	41-12	58-43	696	34.11	SW-4	Slight Sea
" 5	45-03	41-42	801	35.60	SW-4	Moderate Sea
" 6	49-04	22-41	814	36.17	Var-5	Moderate Sea
" 7	49-49	01-14	833	36.21	Var-5	Bishop Rock abeam 6:16 a.m., BST
" 7			47	33.57	Var-5	Arrived Havre L. V. 1:24 p.m., BST

Passage Ambrose L. V. to Bishop Rock:
3 Days, 10 Hours, 40 Minutes — Average Speed: 35.59 Knots

Total Distance, NEW YORK to LE HAVRE: 3,191 Miles
Steaming Time: 3 Days, 17 Hours, 48 Minutes — Average Speed: 33.53 Knots

NOTE: A Nautical Mile is approximately 15 per cent longer than a Statute or Land Mile

These passages are world records. It is the first time in a century that an American ship has captured the Blue Ribbon of the North Atlantic. The United States Lines is rightfully proud of the achievement.

MAIDEN VOYAGE
QUADRUPLE SCREW TURBINE STEAMER
UNITED STATES
Commodore Harry Manning
Captain, U. S. N. R.

Abstract of Log　　　　　　　　　　　　　　　　　　**Voyage 1, Westbound**

From SOUTHAMPTON to NEW YORK, via LE HAVRE

Left Nab Tower, 5:00 p.m., BST, July 10, 1952　　　Arrived Havre L. V., 7:24 p.m., BST, July 10, 1952
Distance, Nab Tower to Le Havre L. V.: 75 miles
Steaming Time: 2 Hours, 24 Minutes — Average Speed: 31.25 Knots

DATE	LAT. N.	LONG. W.	NAUT. MILES	SPEED	WIND	REMARKS
July 11						Departure Havre L. V., 2:00 a.m., BST
" 11	49-49	08-49	341	34.10	W-5	Abeam Bishop Rock 9:17 a.m., BST
" 12	48-10	31-35	902	36.08	W-3	Moderate Sea
" 13	42-56	50-43	865	33.92	Var-2	Light fog; speed reduced
" 14	40-26	69-51	872	34.19	Var-1	Smooth Sea, Hazy
" 14			175			Arrived Ambrose L. V., 4:29 p.m., EDT

Passage, Bishop Rock to Ambrose L. V.: 2906 Miles
3 Days, 12 Hours, 12 Minutes — Average Speed: 34.51 Knots

Total Distance, Le Havre to New York: 3155 Miles
Steaming Time: 3 Days, 19 Hours, 29 Minutes — Average Speed: 34.48 Knots

NOTE: A Nautical Mile is approximately 15 per cent longer than a Statute or Land Mile

These passages are world records. It is the first time in a century that an American ship has captured the Blue Ribbon of the North Atlantic for both East and West passages. The United States Lines is rightfully proud of the achievement. We believe you are too.

(Records courtesy of Maritime Industry Museum at Fort Schuyler)

- *S.S. United States* Foundation was officially chartered as a non-profit organization in March, 1998. For more information contact

    Robert H. Westover, Chairman
    S.S. United States Foundation
    P.O. Box 853
    Washington, D.C. 20044
    Tel: 703-625-3037

Commodore Alexanderson's Graduation Record from New York State Merchant Marine Academy

RECORD AT GRADUATION
DECK

ADAPTABILITY .... *V.G*

SEAMANSHIP .... *good*

RULES OF THE ROAD ..... *V.G*

SHIP STABILITY .... *good*

CARGO STOWAGE .... *good*

SMALL BOAT HANDLING .... *good*

NAVIGATION, THEORETICAL .... *good*

NAVIGATIONI, PRACTICAL .... *good*

PILOTING .... *good*

SHIPS BUSINESS .... *good*

SIGNALS, FLAG .... *good*

       SEMAPHORE .... *good*

       BLINKER .... *good*

STEAM ENGINERING ....

AGE ... **19"** ... CHEST ... **99"**

HEIGHT ... **70 3/4** ... HAIR ... **dk. br.**

WEIGHT ... **164 1/2** ... EYES ... **gray**

Courtesy of Maritime Industry Museum at Fort Schuyler.

GLOSSAR Y OF NAUTICAL TERMS

Battleship: Any of a class of large warships with the biggest guns and very heavy armor. These ships are also called, "battlewagons."

Boilers: A steel or iron container housed in a steamship in which water is boiled or heated to give the ship's engines power.

Bow: The front part of a ship; prow.

Bridge/Bridge-Wing: A raised platform on a ship for the commanding officer.

Brig: A prison or jail on a naval or merchant vessel.

Bulkheads: Any of the upright partitions separating parts of a ship for protection against fire or leakage.

Captain: The commander or master of a ship.

C.O.: Commanding officer of a ship or any military unit or group.

Commodoress: The feminine term of commodore; an officer ranking above captain in the U.S. Navy.

Crew: The personnel of a ship, except the officers.

Designer: A person who designs or makes original sketches such as those of a ship.

Engine Room: A place in the bottom of a ship or boat where the engines are housed.

Fireboats: A boat equipped with fire fighting equipment, used along waterfronts.

Frigate: A U. S. warship larger than a destroyer and smaller than a light cruiser.

Hales Trophy: The trophy given to a ship that breaks the record for the fastest transatlantic ocean crossing.

Hull: The frame or body of a ship.

Knots: A term for a unit of speed of one nautical mile an hour (equivalent to 6,076.12 feet).

Laid Up: A nautical term used for a ship that is not in service any longer.

Life-Ring: A buoyant circular device for saving a person's life from drowning by keeping his/her body afloat.

Luxury Liner: A steamship in regular service that carries passengers from one destination to the other.

Maiden Voyage: The first sea voyage of a ship or boat.

Memorabilia: Items or things from a ship worth remembering or collecting.

Mothballed: A term given to a ship or ships that are no longer used.

Naval Base: A center of operations or source of supply for navy ships; headquarters.

Naval Reserve: Navy forces or personnel not on active duty but subject to call.

Pennant Flags: Any long narrow flags flown from a ship.

Pier: A structure built out over water and supported by pillars.

Radar Mast: A tall mast of a ship which houses systems used for sending out and receiving radio waves used to navigate the ship.

Retired Fleet: A number of warships that are not used any longer and are anchored together.

NEW CHILDREN'S BOOK ABOUT THE S.S. *UNITED STATES* WILL BE AVAILABLE BY LATE SUMMER! FILL OUT THE INFORMATION BELOW TO RESERVE YOUR COPY!

The illustration above, which is taken from the book, shows Jon receiving a model of the ship in celebration of his seventh birthday. The gift is from his grandfather, Commodore L.J. Alexanderson.

The above photo by Ian Shiffman, Table Bay Underway Shipping, shows the "BIG U" during her heyday years 1952 - 1969.

A new children's book about the *S.S. UNITED STATES* will be available late this summer! To reserve your copy, fill out the information below and mail to the address below along with a check.

The story, written by E.B. Fletcher and illustrated by Wendy Bruce, is an historical fiction piece about a young boy, Jon, and his fascination with the abandoned, aging ocean liner, *S.S. UNITED STATES*. Jon lives in Philadelphia, where the ship is moored, and is astonished to find that his own grandfather, Commodore L.J. Alexanderson, was the ship's last captain! After some prodding, grandfather takes Jon aboard the stripped ship for a tour. The Commodore is very saddened to see the ship's deteriorated condition. Jon, however, thinks the ship is wonderful and is thrilled to finally be aboard! The story has many lessons hidden within its pages. In the end, Jon asks the question, "Could paradise be on the bridge of a ship?"

The hard bound book, printed by Dietz Press, is for any elementary school age child. It contains web sites, maps, defined nautical terms, a cut away model of the ship and MUCH, MUCH MORE!